W9-BDF-949

Conrad

Saves Pinger Park

MARIMBA BOOKS
An imprint of The Hudson Publishing Group LLC
356 Glenwood Avenue, East Orange, New Jersey

Text copyright © 2010 by Carvin Winans. Illustrations copyright © 2010 by Illustrations by Leslie Harrington.

All rights reserved. No part of this book may be reproduced in any form or by any means without the prior written consent of the publisher, excepting brief quotes used in reviews.

Special book excerpts or customized printings can also be created to fit specific needs.
For details, write or phone the office of the Marimba special sales manager:

Marimba Books, 356 Glenwood Avenue, East Orange, New Jersey 07017, 973 672-7701
MARIMBA BOOKS and the Marimba Books logo are trademarks of The Hudson Publishing Group LLC.

ISBN-13: 978-1-60349-024-5   ISBN-10: 1-60349-024-8

10 9 8 7 6 5 4 3 2 1

Printed in Canada

In the little town of Pinger
is a very lovely park.
Where all the little children play
But never after dark.

Pinger Park has everything
a child could ever wish.
From monkey bars to bumper cars,
to animals and fish.

There's lots of green, green grass
and sky high tall trees.
Veggie gardens and lovely flowers.
It is *the* place to be.

There's something else in Pinger Town
not far from Pinger Park.
The Zinger family: Mom, Dad, Billy
and a little dog named Spark.

The Zingers' youngest boy,
the one with a freckled face,
is little Conrad, glasses bright
wearing sneakers with no lace.

All the kids loved Conrad,
the way he'd wear his clothes.
His baseball cap turned front to back,
those freckles on his nose.

All the kids around the block
would gather every day
outside his house and holler out,
"Hey Conrad, come and play."

Conrad and his friends
took pride in keeping Pinger Park clean.

They picked up trash and litter.
They were the clean-up team.

One day the Mayor of Pinger called a meeting of the town. "The park has got to go!" he said. "It must be torn down."

Before

After

PINGER PARK

Pinger Tower

Pinger Plaza

"So many families have moved here.
People are coming still.
We need the land the park is on.
There's no land on which to build."

When Conrad and his friends heard this,
it made them very sad.
Without Pinger Park what would they do?
The news was very bad.

Conrad had to think fast.
He told his pals, "here's what I'll do.
I'll write a letter to the city paper
And get it in the news."

So Conrad wrote from his heart
with hope and a very big wish.
And when he finished the letter
it read something like this.

Dear Mr. Mayor,

It's Conrad here.
I'm not sure what I should say.
Some years ago I asked my mom,
"Can I please go out and play?"

Me.
Six year old.

She took me to Pinger Park.
I was only about three.
But I remember it so well.
It was the best fun to me!

The park's where I lost my first tooth.
It's special can't you see?
It's also the place my pals and I
planted our very first tree.

So I write for all of us kids.
I write for the place where we play.
I write for the trees and flowers.
Please let Pinger Park stay."

Everyone read Conrad's letter.
Then they marched to see the Mayor.
"Save Pinger Park!" they chanted.
"Mr. Mayor, don't you care?"

The Mayor was moved with compassion.
He said, "I won't let the park be torn down."
"It means too much to our children.
It means too much to our town."

"So I've made a new decision.
And it comes straight from the heart.
Let's all thank Conrad.
He helped save Pinger Park."

So in the little town of Pinger
there is still a lovely park.
Where all the little children play,
but never after dark.

Pinger Park has everything,
even a new children's bank.
And everyone in Pinger Town,
has Conrad Zinger to thank.

GREEN TIPS FOR YOUR COMMUNITY

- **Set out cans and bottles for neighborhood pickup.**
  (Use your hands to set out cans for pickup by the recycling man.)

- **Choose and recycle rechargeable batteries.**
  (Rechargeable batteries—it's the way to keep your toys and games in play.)

- **Turn off lights in house when not needed.**
  (To save on energy here's what can be done: open the shades and let in the sun.)

- **Don't let the water run when brushing your teeth.**
  (To turn off the water when brushing makes sense; only use water when it is time to rinse.)

- **Walk whenever possible.**
  (Need to go to the store or just mail a letter? Use your feet and walk,
  it will make you feel better.)

- **Recycle newspapers, magazines and junk mail.**
  (Recycling paper can be fun and neat. If you put it in bins then it stays off the streets.)

- Plant a garden or a tree.
(The more we plant trees, the better we breathe.)

- Build a bird house or bird feeder for your backyard.
(Feeding the birds is a nice thing to do. They'll grow to be strong and healthy like you.)

- Unplug game systems and computers when not in use.
(Just pull the plug when the games are not on, and plug them back when it's time for more fun.)

- Use community resources.
(Libraries are good places for spending your time, with all sorts of books to strengthen your mind.)

- Celebrate Earth Day in your community each year.
(Make a personal commitment with a group of friends and celebrate Earth Day from beginning to end.)

All these tips can be used to protect the planet!

Carvin Winans

is a singer and Grammy award-winning songwriter. Following in the footsteps of his parents, he began performing at the age of four and gained fame as a member of the Gospel group, The Winans. Now turning his lifelong gift for writing to children's books, the father of six says "God has truly blessed me with gifts to share with the world, and as far as I'm concerned, I've only just begun." *Conrad Saves Pinger Park* is his first book for children. Carvin says, *"I dedicate this book to my Lord and Saviour Jesus Christ, my beautiful wife, Chérie Winans, and my wonderful children, Carvin Jr., Juan, his wife Lisa, Joy, Ian, Shanniah, and Laylah. In memory of my Dad, David "Pop" Winans Sr."*

Leslie Harrington

says her work as an artist is best described by the phrase "draw with a pencil, paint with a mouse." After earning a BFA in Illustration from The Columbus College of Art & Design, she worked for several years as a background painter in the children's videogame industry. Now a fulltime illlustrator, she uses pencil and PhotoShop to create the vibrant illustrations that have been published in Highlights Magazine and several educational books. *Conrad Saves Pinger Park* is her first published picture book.